趣味漫畫學英語

小學漫畫英語王

Prepositions
介詞

新雅文化事業有限公司
www.sunya.com.hk

介詞（prepositions）很難學？
不用怕，由零開始教曉你！

本書主題

全書以介詞為主題，共有 60 個單元，把介詞劃分 10 個類別，方便學童分類學習，輕鬆提升英語能力！

時間 1　at

漫畫看一看

Don't forget to come tomorrow. I want to see you again.

Sure. When should we meet?

Well, let's meet at 3 o'clock.

All right. See you at 3 in the afternoon tomorrow. Bye!

See you!

I will ask Lion King to come with me.

10

英語介詞你要知

介詞解讀與辨析

時間介詞 at 表示一時一刻、非常短促的時間，一般用於特定時刻。什麼是特定時刻？一時正、二時正是特定時刻，午飯、晚餐、日出、日落也是特定時刻。

實用例句齊來學

at
- I always get up at 7 o'clock.
  我平常七時起牀。
- Will it get cold at night?
  夜間天氣會轉涼嗎？
- They set out at sunset for a night's fishing.
  他們日落時分出海，準備夜間捕魚。
- I saw him this morning at breakfast.
  我今天早上吃早餐時看到了他。
- Dad likes to listen to the radio at bedtime.
  爸爸喜歡在睡前聽收音機。

增測知識大放送

介詞短語 at present、at the moment 及 at the same time 都是特定時刻。例如：
- Sorry, he's not here at the moment.
  對不起，他現在不在還見。

以下情況則屬例外，用 in，不用 at，包括 in the morning、in the afternoon 和 in the evening。例如：
- She usually does exercises in the morning / afternoon.
  她通常在早上／下午做運動。

11

漫畫看一看

每個單元以趣味漫畫帶出 1 至 3 個重點介詞，孩子透過閱讀漫畫，可學懂如何正確運用介詞，形式生動有趣，自主閱讀沒難度。

英語介詞你要知

本書把介詞劃分為以下 10 個類別，內容豐富實用，學習事半功倍。

1 時間　　　　2 位置　　　　3 方向
4 施行者　　　5 工具　　　　6 對立 / 讓步
7 組成部分　　8 計算　　　　9 原因 / 目的
10 方式

正文最後更附 10 課常見介詞實例，逐一拆解常犯錯誤。

每個單元均有簡單易明的文字解說，包括 3 個欄目：

① 📣 介詞解讀與辨析

從意義和用法兩大角度，說明介詞和介詞片語的必學知識點，迅速幫助孩子學習介詞，掌握其運用，打好英文基礎。

② ★ 實用例句齊來學

收錄大量實用地道的雙語例句，示範介詞在具體情境中的正確用法，同時鼓勵讀者多看多讀，消化學習，模仿應用。

③ 🔍 增潤知識大放送

囊括拼寫、語法、相反詞、替代詞、慣用語等增潤知識，循序漸進培養英文語感。

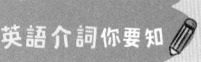

英語介詞你要知

介詞解讀與辨析
on 表示「在……的表面上」，用於平面或比一點為大的空間。

★ 實用例句齊來學

on
- Write your answer on page 10.
  在第十頁寫上答案。
- Let's sit down on the ground.
  我們坐在地上吧。
- There are no prices on this menu.
  這份餐牌上沒有標示價錢。
- There was a "no smoking" sign on the wall.
  牆上貼有「不准吸煙」的告示。
- The old woman was sitting on a rocking chair.
  那老婦坐在一張搖椅上。

🔍 增潤知識大放送
平面的空間還包括 on your face、on the floor、on a table、on the grass 等，例如：
- He had a puzzled look on his face.
  他一臉困惑不解。

但以下情況則屬例外，用 in，不用 on：
- He was looking at his reflection in a mirror.
  他正看著自己在鏡中的影像。
- Sometimes he has breakfast in bed.
  有時候他在牀上吃早餐。
- Have you read that news in the newspaper?
  你在報紙上看到了那則新聞嗎？

29

練習室

末附設6個練習，蓋本書內容，動動筋，學以致用，自檢測學習成果。

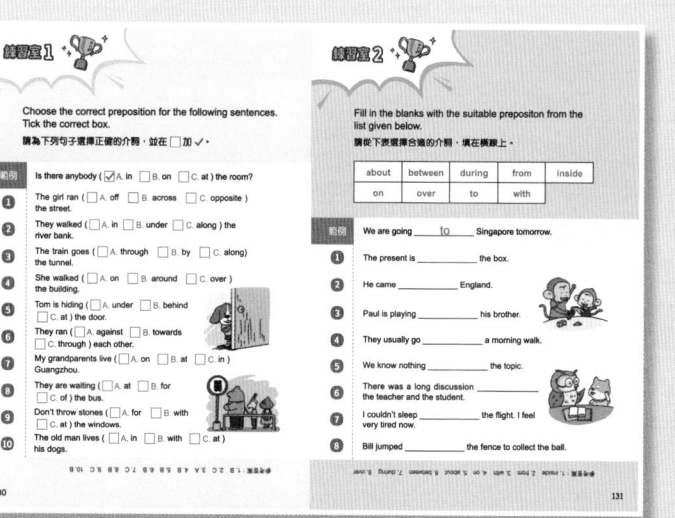

練習室 1 🏆

Choose the correct preposition for the following sentences. Tick the correct box.

請為下列句子選擇正確的介詞，並在 ☐ 加 ✓。

範例 Is there anybody (✓A. in ☐ B. on ☐ C. at) the room?

1. The girl ran (☐ A. off ☐ B. across ☐ C. opposite) the street.
2. They walked (☐ A. in ☐ B. under ☐ C. along) the river bank.
3. The train goes (☐ A. through ☐ B. by ☐ C. along) the tunnel.
4. She walked (☐ A. on ☐ B. around ☐ C. over) the building.
5. Tom is hiding (☐ A. under ☐ B. behind ☐ C. at) the door.
6. They ran (☐ A. against ☐ B. towards ☐ C. through) each other.
7. My grandparents live (☐ A. on ☐ B. at ☐ C. in) Guangzhou.
8. They are waiting (☐ A. at ☐ B. for ☐ C. of) the bus.
9. Don't throw stones (☐ A. for ☐ B. with ☐ C. at) the windows.
10. The old man lives (☐ A. in ☐ B. with ☐ C. at) his dogs.

參考答案： 1.B 2.C 3.A 4.B 5.B 6.B 7.C 8.B 9.C 10.B

130

練習室 2 🏆

Fill in the blanks with the suitable prepositon from the list given below.

請從下表選擇合適的介詞，填在橫線上。

about	between	during	from	inside
on	over	to	with	

範例 We are going ___to___ Singapore tomorrow.

1. The present is _____ the box.
2. He came _____ England.
3. Paul is playing _____ his brother.
4. They usually go _____ a morning walk.
5. We know nothing _____ the topic.
6. There was a long discussion _____ the teacher and the student.
7. I couldn't sleep _____ the flight. I feel very tired now.
8. Bill jumped _____ the fence to collect the ball.

參考答案： 1. inside 2. from 3. with 4. on 5. about 6. between 7. during 8. over

131

作者的話

　　英語的詞彙數以萬計，相比之下，介詞所佔的比例很小，只有一百多個，但可說是英語中最活躍的詞類。我們在學習英語的過程中經常會碰到介詞，它們的使用範圍之廣、使用頻率之高，以及使用難度之大，恐怕也是其他詞類所不及的。

　　介詞的英漢差異很大，大到有時候讓我們難以在中文裏找到與之對應的介詞。簡單舉個例子：Of the people, by the people, for the people. 這是美國第十六任總統林肯的一句名言，今天我們看到的翻譯多是「民有、民治、民享」，但為何介詞 of、by、for 翻譯成中文時，要換成動詞「有」、「治」、「享」呢？那是因為我們無法在中文裏找到對等的介詞。

　　如果介詞只是英漢差異大，而不佔重要地位，我們大可不需特別理會。但是介詞偏偏很重要，除了是因為使用頻率高，詞義比較空泛卻變化多端，還因為它的結構功能強。我們知道句子是有結構的，句子結構就像是房子的鋼筋混凝土框架，普通單詞如名詞、動詞、形容詞等，就像是一塊塊磚，填充到這框架裏去。介詞雖然也是單詞，卻不是單純的填充進句子，而是參與了句子結構的構成，直接影響句子的意思。

　　我們舉個例子來說明：The magician is walking on a rope, with an owl standing on his shoulder. 如把句子翻譯成中文，大概就是：魔術師走在一根繩子上，肩上站着一隻

貓頭鷹。值得注意的是，當中的介詞 with 並沒有恰當的中文對應成分，但它在句子裏扮演着舉足輕重的角色，連接了主句和獨立主格的結構，是整個句子的框架。

英語難學好，其中一個主要原因其實是來自介詞。很多學生使用英語時，往往會犯下遺漏介詞或誤用介詞的錯誤，因此，各類英語考試均有這方面的測試內容。能夠好好掌握介詞的用法，確實是學好英語的關鍵所在。介詞其實也不難學，只是需要一些方法培養我們的敏感度。本書便是針對小學生這方面的需要而設計，有以下四大特色：

第一，全書 60 課，精要地闡釋各種介詞和介詞片語的意義和用法。

第二，每課均收錄大量例句，務求透過簡明實用的例子，讓小學生懂得如何運用介詞。

第三，一些例外情況或容易混淆、錯誤使用的介詞更會提供補充說明，講解其於文法上的正確用法和注意事項，提供增潤知識，幫助讀者加強運用介詞的能力。

第四，書後附設 6 個練習，供讀者測試水平，發揮所學。

Aman Chiu

什麼是介詞？
What are prepositions?

　　介詞又叫前置詞，是英語的重要組成部分，介詞「介」於兩個詞之間，用來表示兩個詞的某種聯繫，例如在時間、空間或文法上的關係。

介詞的種類

英語的介詞從 **字形** 上區分，有以下兩類：

❶ 簡單介詞，即只由一個單詞構成，例如：

at	in	on	inside	into
of	by	with	without	about

❷ 短語介詞，即由兩個或以上的單詞構成，例如：

because of	out of	instead of
in front of	rather than	in spite of

如把介詞按 **詞義** 分類，一般包括以下五類：

❶ 時間介詞，常見的介詞包括 at、on 和 in，例如：

at ten o'clock	on Sunday	in January
at lunch time	on my birthday	in the morning

❷ 位置介詞，常見的介詞包括 at、on 和 in，例如：

at the bus stop	on the wall	in a car
at the entrance	on a table	in the library

❸ 方向介詞，常見的介詞包括 to、through 和 into，例如：

go to school	drive through a tunnel
jump into the pool	

❹ 表示施行者的介詞，介詞例子包括 by 和 with，例如：

[a book] written by Shakespeare
[a football field] filled with fans

❺ 表示工具的介詞，例如：by 和 with，例如：

by car	with a hammer

　　其他介詞類別還有對立或讓步、組成部分、計算、原因或目的，以及方式。值得注意的是，有些介詞身兼多重角色，在不同語境下產生不同意思，例如 at、on、in，既是時間介詞，又是位置介詞；又如 by 和 with，既是表示施行者的介詞，又是表示工具的介詞。

Contents 目錄 （按介詞詞義分類）

漫畫看一看

Don't forget to come tomorrow. I want to see you again.

Sure. When should we meet?

All right. See you at 3 in the afternoon tomorrow. Bye!

See you!

Well, let's meet at 3 o'clock.

I will ask Lion King to come with me.

介詞解讀與辨析

時間介詞 at 表示一時一刻、非常短促的時間,一般用於特定時刻。什麼是特定時刻?一時正、二時正是特定時刻,午飯、晚餐、日出、日落也是特定時刻。

★ 實用例句齊來學

at

- I always get up **at** 7 o'clock.
  我平常七時起牀。

- Will it get cold **at** night?
  夜間天氣會轉涼嗎?

- They set out **at** sunset for a night's fishing.
  他們日落時分出海,準備夜間捕魚。

- I saw him this morning **at** breakfast.
  我今天早上吃早餐時看到了他。

- Dad likes to listen to the radio **at** bedtime.
  爸爸喜歡在睡前聽收音機。

增潤知識大放送

介詞短語 at present、at the moment 及 at the same time 都是特定時刻。例如:

- Sorry, he's not here **at the moment**.
  對不起,他現在不在這兒。

以下情況則屬例外,用 in,不用 at,包括 in the morning、in the afternoon 和 in the evening。例如:

- She usually does exercises **in the morning / afternoon**.
  她通常在早上 / 下午做運動。

🔊 介詞解讀與辨析

時間介詞 on 一般用於日期和特定日子。日期指特定的年、月、日,或一周裏的某天;特定日子包括一年裏不同的節慶、假期。

★ 實用例句齊來學

on

- Lily was born **on** January the first.
  莉莉在一月一日出生。

- This museum is usually closed **on** Tuesdays.
  這博物館通常在星期二閉館。

- We will throw a party **on** Christmas Eve.
  我們將在平安夜舉行派對。

- Charles won three medals **on** sports day.
  查理斯在運動日贏了三枚獎牌。

🔍 增潤知識大放送

有些特定日子除外,用 at,不用 on,包括 at the weekend、at Easter 和 at Christmas。例如:

- We get a week off school **at Easter**.
  復活節我們學校放假一周。

表示將來某個時間,next 前面無需用 on。例如:

- I'll see you **next** Monday.
  我下星期一見你。

yesterday 和 tomorrow 前面也不用 on,例如:

- I ran into John **yesterday**.
  我昨天無意中遇上約翰。

- See you **tomorrow**.
  明天見。

13

漫畫看一看

🔊 介詞解讀與辨析

時間介詞 in 一般用於星期、月份、季節、年份、年代、世紀或更長的時間。

⭐ 實用例句齊來學

in

- Jack's birthday is **in** October.
  傑克在十月生日。

- It usually snows here **in** the winter.
  這裏冬天通常會下雪。

- The modern Olympics began **in** 1896.
  現代奧運會始於 1896 年。

- How did people dress **in** the 60s?
  六十年代的人是怎麼穿衣服的？

- This temple was built **in** the 12th century.
  這座廟建於十二世紀。

- Were there dinosaurs **in** the Ice Age?
  冰河時期有恐龍嗎？

🔍 增潤知識大放送

表示過去某個時間，last 前面無需用 in。例如：
- We went to Taipei **last** June. 我們去年六月去了台北。

this 和 that 前面也不用 in。例如：
- We'll go camping **this** summer. 我們這個夏天會去露營。

表示過去和將來，則需用 in。例如：
- Life was very difficult **in** the past. 過去生活很艱難。

- I'll have to be more careful **in** future. 今後我得小心點。

漫畫看一看

Where's my bike? I put it here last night. It's gone now!

I heard some strange noises in the night. Someone must have stolen it.

There have been at least ten robberies recently. People don't go out at night now.

Let's report to the police.

Sure!

16

📢 介詞解讀與辨析

at night 的意思是 during any night，泛指任何一個晚上。

in the night 的意思是 during one particular night，特指某一個晚上。

⭐ 實用例句齊來學

at night

- It gets cold **at night**. 夜間天氣轉涼。

- I never play computer games **at night**. 我晚上從不玩電腦遊戲。

- This park is quite dangerous **at night**. 這個公園晚上很危險。

in the night

- Someone stole his bicycle **in the night**.
  有人在夜裏偷了他的單車。

- I was awake **in the night**, thinking about the school picnic last week.
  我在夜裏醒來，想着上周的學校旅行。

🔍 增潤知識大放送

我們説 in the morning、in the afternoon、in the evening 和 at night，來泛指一天的時段。例如：

- She usually jogs **in the morning**. 她通常在早上慢跑。

- She seldom swims **at night**. 她很少在夜間游泳。

evening 和 night 不同，evening 是「傍晚、晚間」，尤其指下午六時到晚上十時，它的反義詞是 morning。night 是「夜晚、黑夜」，尤其指晚上十時打後的深夜，它的反義詞是 day。

on time, in time

漫畫看一看

介詞解讀與辨析

on time 指「準時、按時」完成某事。

in time 則指「及時」,即是在某時間或限期前完成某事。

實用例句齊來學

on time

- The high-speed trains usually arrive **on time**.
  高速列車通常準時到達。

- David did not hand in his homework **on time**.
  大衞沒有按時交功課。

in time

- The ambulance arrived **in time**.
  救護車及時到達。

- We arrived **in time** for the concert.
  我們在演唱會開始前到達。

- I got to school just **in time** — it's starting to rain.
  我及時趕到學校,隨後就開始下雨了。

增潤知識大放送

on time 前可加 right 或 dead 來加強語氣,例如:

- The bus arrived **right on time**. 巴士極為準時到達了。

in time 中間可插入 plenty of 來加強語氣,例如:

- We got to the station **in plenty of time**. 我們一早就到了車站。

慣用語 in no time 指「很快地」,意思等同 very quickly,例如:

- The children ate the snacks **in no time**.
  那些孩子很快吃完了小吃。

past, to

介詞解讀與辨析

past 和 to 用於報時，用以回答 What's the time now? 或 What time is it? 這些問題。

past 表示時間「晚於；過」；to 表示時間「在……之前；差」。兩者在用法上的區別可見於以下口訣：1 to 30 PAST, over 30 TO（1 到 30 用 past；超過 30 用 to）。

★ 實用例句齊來學

past

- It's five **past** five. 時間是 5 時 5 分。
- It's twenty-two **past** five. 時間是 5 時 22 分。
- It was a quarter **past** three. 時間是 3 時 15 分。

to

- It's ten **to** nine. 時間是 8 時 50 分。
- It's twenty-two **to** five. 時間是 4 時 38 分。
- It was a quarter **to** three. 時間是 2 時 45 分。

增潤知識大放送

to 用於分針過了 6 但未到 12 的時間，即是 31 分至 59 分，變相就要倒數，但小時上要用下一個數字，例如「6 時 35 分」會說成 twenty-five to seven，切忌說成 twenty-five to six。

past 可用於代詞 half 之後，但 to 不能用在代詞 half 之後。例如：
- It was **half past** eight. 時間是 8 時 30 分。

漫畫看一看

Mum, I'm very hungry now!

Why?

I haven't eaten anything for hours. I am now "the very hungry caterpillar".

THE VERY HUNGRY CATERPILLAR

I'm hungry, too. I've not eaten anything since breakfast.

Okay. Food is almost ready. Wait a minute.

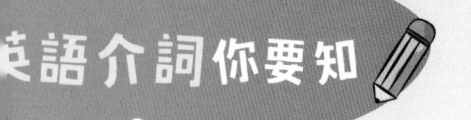

介詞解讀與辨析

since 和 for 都是用來表示時間的長度。

since 接時間點，比如具體的年、月、日等，表示從過去某個具體時間起，一直延續到現在。

for 接一段時間，比如幾年、幾個月、幾個小時等，表示某事延續，維持一段時間。

實用例句齊來學

since

- I haven't seen him **since** last Christmas.
  自去年聖誕節起，我一直沒有見過他了。

- They have lived in Sydney **since** 2000.
  自 2000 年起，他們就住在悉尼。

for

- I haven't seen him **for** half a year.
  我半年沒有見過他了。

- They have lived in Sydney **for** almost twenty years.
  他們住在悉尼差不多二十年了。

增潤知識大放送

since 多與現在完成式 (present perfect tense) 連用，說明了從 since 後的時間開始，直到現在說話時，狀態和行為仍在持續。

同樣地，for 多與現在完成式或過去完成式 (past perfect tense) 連用，但也可用於任何時態。例如：

- Bake the cake **for** thirty minutes. 把蛋糕焗半個小時。
- We chatted **for** quite a while. 我們聊了好一會兒。

漫畫看一看

Hey, sweetie, how was school today?

Mum, during I was at school, I met several nice friends.

Did you say during your time at school, you met several nice friends?

Yes, that's what I meant. And they're very nice to me.

Great! Tell me more about them.

介詞解讀與辨析

during 指「在……期間」，用來表示一個動作在另外一個相關事件中持續的時段。during 後面需要接名詞或名詞片語，而不是句子，一般放在句子中間，也可放於句子開首，以作強調。

★ 實用例句齊來學

during

- Don't play on your phone **during** the meal. 吃飯時別滑手機。
- You're not allowed to talk **during** the exam. 考試時不可交談。
- I heard a loud noise **during** the night. 夜裏我聽見一聲巨響。
- **During** the Christmas holidays, we went to Beijing.
  聖誕節假期，我們去了北京。
- **During** the summer season, all the hotels here are full.
  整個夏季，這裏的所有酒店都客滿。

增潤知識大放送

during 不可以用來表示持續的時段或時間的長度，例如我們不能説：Anna has lived in Hong Kong during five years. 而要説：Anna has lived in Hong Kong for five years. （安娜在香港生活了五年。）

雖然 during 與 while 都指「在……期間」，但前者是介詞，而後者則是連接詞。所以，during 後面不可接子句，而 while 則可以。例如我們不能説：John came during we were having dinner. 而要説：John came while we were having dinner.
（我們吃晚餐時，約翰來了。）

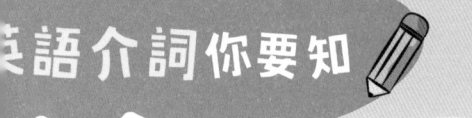

英語介詞你要知

🔍 介詞解讀與辨析

介詞 at 指「在……裏；在……旁」或「處於某地方」，用來表示地點或位置，一般用於特定的定點位置、相對細小的空間。

⭐ 實用例句齊來學

at

- The bakery is **at** the end of the street.
  麵包店在街道的盡頭。

- The kitten came and lay down **at** my feet.
  小貓走了過來，趴在我的腳邊。

- Daisy is waiting for you **at** the bus stop.
  黛絲正在巴士站那裏等你。

- We'll meet you **at** the entrance of the mall.
  我們會在商場的入口跟你碰面。

🔎 增潤知識大放送

常見的介詞短語包括 at work、at school 和 at home。例如：

- Are you **at home**?
  你在家裏嗎？

- Dad is still **at work**.
  爸爸還在上班。

at 表示的方位是一個點，就像地圖上的建築物，沒有裏外之分，也不考慮其空間結構。例如：

- See you **at the park**. 我們公園見。

比較以下例句，in the park 表示在公園這個空間的裏面，公園被視為一個空間，而不是一個點。

- See you **in the park**. 我們在公園裏見。

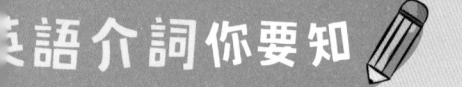

介詞解讀與辨析

on 表示「在……的表面上」,用於平面或比一點為大的空間。

★ 實用例句齊來學

on

- Write your answer on page 10.
  在第十頁寫上答案。

- Let's sit down on the ground.
  我們坐在地上吧。

- There are no prices on this menu.
  這份餐牌上沒有標示價錢。

- There was a "no smoking" sign on the wall.
  牆上貼有「不准吸煙」的告示。

- The old woman was sitting on a rocking chair.
  那老婦坐在一張搖椅上。

增潤知識大放送

平面的空間還包括 on your face、on the floor、on a table、on the grass 等,例如:

- He had a puzzled look on his face.
  他一臉困惑不解。

但以下情況則屬例外,用 in,不用 on:

- He was looking at his reflection in a mirror.
  他正看着自己在鏡中的影像。

- Sometimes he has breakfast in bed.
  有時候他在牀上吃早餐。

- Have you read that news in the newspaper?
  你在報紙上看到了那則新聞嗎?

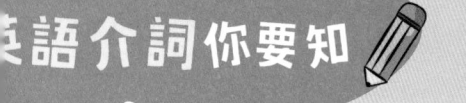

📢 介詞解讀與辨析

in 指「在某處」或「在⋯⋯裏面；在（立體空間）內」，用於圍住的或較大的空間。

✦ 實用例句齊來學

in

- They live **in** a large old house. 他們住在一間古老大屋內。
- Dad is still **in** the office. 爸爸仍在辦公室裏。
- The children are playing **in** the garden. 孩子在花園裏玩耍。
- Do you live **in** Canada? 你住在加拿大嗎？
- Jupiter is **in** the Solar System. 木星位於太陽系內。

🔍 增潤知識大放送

圍住的空間還包括一些交通工具，例如 in a car / taxi / boat / helicopter 等：

- I left my bag **in the car**. 我把袋遺漏在車裏了。
- They crossed the river **in a boat**. 他們乘小船過河。
- What's it really like flying **in a helicopter**?
  坐直升機的感覺是怎樣的呢？

以下情況則屬例外，用 on，不用 in，例如 on a bus / train / plane / ship 等：

- Smoking is not allowed **on the bus**. 巴士上不准吸煙。
- There may be a bomb **on the plane**! 航班上可能有炸彈！
- People said there's a ghost **on the ship**. 人們說船上有鬼。

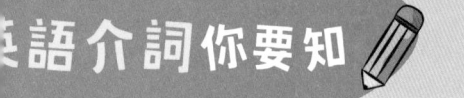  

英語介詞你要知

介詞解讀與辨析

corner 可以搭配介詞 at 或 in。

如表達建築物、馬路、街的轉角處,用 at。

如表達在一個空間內的轉角處,則用 in。

⭐ 實用例句齊來學

at the corner

- We are **at the corner** of the coffee shop.
  我們在咖啡店的轉角處。

- Let's meet **at the corner** of North Street and East Road.
  我們在北街和東路的拐角處碰面吧。

in the corner

- The spider is building a web **in the corner**.
  蜘蛛在牆角結網。

- "Please stand **in the corner**!" said the teacher.
  老師說:「請站到牆角去。」

🔍 增潤知識大放送

on the corner 指「在一個平面上的轉角處」,例如:

- Don't put your cup **on the corner** of the table.
  不要把杯子放在桌子的角落。

- There is a postbox **on the corner**. 街角處有個郵箱。

慣用語 around the corner 則指「就在附近」,也可引申指時間上的「即將到來」,例如:

- My best friend lives just **around the corner**.
  我的好友就住在附近。

- My birthday is right **around the corner**. 我的生日快到了。

漫畫看一看

📢 介詞解讀與辨析

arrive 解作「到達；抵達；到來」，作不及物動詞用，不接任何介詞。

相對來説，arrive at 後面通常接「小地點」，如派對、戲院、超級市場、酒店、機場等；arrive in 後面則通常接「大地點」，如城市或國家。

⭐ 實用例句齊來學

arrive at

- The guests have **arrived at** the hotel.
  賓客已經到達酒店。

- We **arrived at** the cinema in time to catch the start of the film.
  我們及時趕到電影院，趕上了電影開場。

arrive in

- We were driving all day and **arrived in** Melbourne after dark.
  我們開了一整天車，天黑後才到達墨爾本。

- I'll give you a call as soon as I **arrive in** Taiwan.
  我一到達台灣就會給你打電話。

🔍 增潤知識大放送

arrive 不接 to，例如我們不説：We arrived to the station.
而説：We arrived at the station.（我們到達車站。）

人們一般説 arrive home，而不説 arrive at home，例如：

- When we **arrived home**, we were exhausted.
  我們回到家裏時，已筋疲力盡。

in front of, behind

漫畫看一看

介詞解讀與辨析

in front of 和 behind 是用來表示前後的位置介詞。

in front of 指在某地點、人物或物件之前。

behind 指在某地點、人物或物件之後。

★ 實用例句齊來學

in front of

- Let's meet **in front of** the cinema. 我們在電影院門口前見面吧。
- There is a swimming pool **in front of** the hotel.
  酒店前有游泳池。
- I couldn't watch the TV because she was standing **in front of** the screen. 我無法看電視，因為她站在熒幕前面。

behind

- She's hiding **behind** the sofa. 她躲在沙發背後。
- A boy ran out from **behind** a tree. 男孩從樹後跑出來。
- The man shut the door **behind** him. 那男人把身後的門關上。

增潤知識大放送

in front of 作為一個介詞片語，of 是必需的；否則它便作副詞來用，解作「前面」。例如：

- The washroom is **in front**. 洗手間在前面。
- The car **in front** stopped suddenly. 前面的車突然停了下來。

介詞 before 與 in front of 同義，都指「在……前面」，in front of 用在普遍的場合，而 before 用於文學與正式場合，例如法庭裏的審訊和教堂裏的儀式等。例如：

- The priest stood **before** the altar. 那位神父站在聖壇前面。

漫畫看一看

It's no joking, but we found a snake nearby!

Really? Where is it?

It's above the cave over there.

What does it look like?

It's huge, and it has stripes all over its body.

It has just swallowed a rabbit!

Let's catch it to avoid being the next victim.

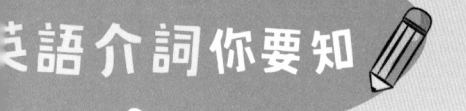

介詞解讀與辨析

above 和 over 都指某物高於另一事物或在另一事物的上方。

above 指「在……上面;在……較高處」。

over 指「直接在……之上」。

實用例句齊來學

above

- A sign hung **above** the door.
  門的上方掛着一塊招牌。

- There is an owl on the branch **above** you.
  在你頭頂上方的樹枝上有一隻貓頭鷹。

over

- There is no bridge **over** the river.
  河上沒有橋。

- Daniel went to sleep with a magazine **over** his face.
  丹尼爾用雜誌蓋着臉睡覺。

增潤知識大放送

above 和 over 的意思相同,常常可以互相替代。例如:

- The birds flew **above** / **over** the trees. 鳥兒在樹叢的上方飛翔。

- The sign **above** / **over** the door says "Danger".
  門上方的牌子上寫着「危險」。

不過,over 還帶有覆蓋表面的含義;而above 僅表示「高於……」的意思,沒有覆蓋表面的含義。在以下語境中,絕對不能用 above 來替代 over。

- Grass is growing **over** the roof. 屋頂長滿了草。

- The magician put a mask **over** his face. 魔術師戴上了面具。

英語介詞你要知

介詞解讀與辨析

below 和 under 同樣指「在⋯⋯下方」，表示某物低於另一事物或在另一事物的下方。

below 指「在某平面之下；在較低處」。
under 指「在⋯⋯下面；在⋯⋯下方」。

★ 實用例句齊來學

below

- A boat is **below** the bridge. 一艘船在橋的下面。
- **Below** us on the right there is the mighty Yellow River.
在我們右下方是浩瀚的黄河。

under

- We sheltered **under** the tree. 我們躲在樹下。
- The boys were hiding **under** the bed.
那些男孩躲在牀底下。

🔍 增潤知識大放送

below 和 under 的意思相同，常常可以互相替代。例如：

- They are sitting **below** / **under** a tree. 他們坐在樹下。

不過，below 並不總是可以替代 under，因為 below 僅表示「低於⋯⋯」的意思，under 則意味着「在⋯⋯的正下方」，例如表示某物被一層東西（如：衣服）覆蓋着。在以下語境中，絕對不能用 below 來替代 under。

- That man has a gun **under** his coat.
那男人在大衣下藏着一枝手槍。
- **Under** the film of fat, the sausages are pink.
一層薄薄的脂肪覆蓋在粉紅色的香腸上。

介詞解讀與辨析

inside 指「在……裏面；在……內部；在室內」，常指物件、人物、動物等處於某封閉的空間之內。

outside 的意思是「在……外面；在室外」，指物件、人物、動物等處於某封閉的空間之外。

★ 實用例句齊來學

inside

- We were waiting **inside** the cinema. 我們在電影院裏面等着。
- Put the money **inside** your wallet. 把錢放進你的錢包內。
- No one was **inside** the building when the fire broke out.
  火災發生時房子裏沒有人。

outside

- It was a sunny day **outside**. 外面陽光普照。
- The children are playing **outside** the door.
  那些孩子正在門外玩耍。
- The shop **outside** our school sells stuffed animals.
  學校外邊那家商店出售毛絨動物玩具 。

增潤知識大放送

不要把 inside 和 outside 拼寫成 insides 和 outsides。

在非正式英語，尤其在美式英語中，可用 inside of 和 outside of。例如：

- I've known him for years, but I've never been **inside of** his house. 我認識他已經好多年，但我從未去過他家裏。
- Put the chair **outside of** the classroom. 將椅子放在課室外。

英語介詞你要知

📢 介詞解讀與辨析

beside 指「在……旁邊」，表示在某人或某物的一邊，特別指緊貼着某人或某物。

與 beside 意思相同的位置介詞是 next to，同樣指「在……旁邊」。

⭐ 實用例句齊來學

beside

- He usually sits **beside** the driver. 他通常坐在司機旁邊。

- The music room is **beside** the computer room.
  音樂室在電腦室旁邊。

- They have a house **beside** the lake.
  他們在湖邊有一棟房子。

next to

- The bank is **next to** the old cinema. 銀行在舊電影院旁邊。

- Can I sit **next to** the window? 我可以靠窗坐嗎？

- There was a really strange woman sitting **next to** me on the bus. 在巴士上有一個很古怪的女人坐在我旁邊。

🔍 增潤知識大放送

beside 與另一個介詞 besides（結尾有 s）容易被人混淆。beside 指 at the side of，即「在……旁邊」；besides 則指 in addition to 或 as well as，即「除……以外」。例如：

- Please stay **besides** her.
  除了她以外，（其餘各位）請留下。

- What other types of sports do you like **besides** badminton?
  除了羽毛球以外，你還喜歡什麼運動嗎？

漫畫看一看

英語介詞你要知

介詞解讀與辨析

若簡單劃分，between 是在兩者之間；among 是在三者或多於三者，即是一羣人或物之間。

★ 實用例句齊來學

between

- On the plane I was sitting **between** two very large men.
  在航班上，我坐在兩個大個子男人之間。

- There is a fence **between** their garden and our garden.
  他們的花園和我們的花園之間有一道籬笆。

among

- We looked for the ball **among** the bushes.
  我們在灌木叢中找那顆球。

- The International Commerce Centre is **among** the tallest skyscrapers in the world.
  環球貿易廣場是全世界最高的摩天大廈之一。

增潤知識大放送

雖說兩者之間用 between，兩者以上用 among，但也有例外，因為兩者主要的差異不是在數量，而是 between 強調個別性，among 強調整體性。例如：

- I have to choose **between** cakes, puddings and ice cream.
  我得從蛋糕、布丁、冰淇淋中挑選一樣。

- I have to choose **among** the desserts.
  我得從各式甜品中挑選一樣。

漫畫看一看

Excuse me, where is the metro station?

See the bakery over there? The metro station is just across from it.

So it's on the opposite side of the street?

Yes. It's opposite the bakery.

I see it. Thank you!

介詞解讀與辨析

介詞 opposite 表示「在……對面；與……相對」的意思，一般用在句子中間，如用於句首時則起強調作用。

★ 實用例句齊來學

opposite

- We sat **opposite** each other.
  我們面對面坐。

- The bus stop is just **opposite** our school.
  巴士站正好就在我們的學校對面。

- The shop **opposite** our office sells bubble milk tea.
  我們辦公樓對面的那家商店售賣珍珠奶茶。

- **Opposite** the grand palace is the crowded slum.
  宏偉的皇宮對面是擠擁的貧民窟。

增潤知識大放送

opposite 後不接 from，例如我們不說：The public library is opposite from the school. 而說：The public library is opposite the school.（公共圖書館在學校對面。）

opposite 後有時可接 to。例如：

- He missed those days when he lived **opposite to** her.
  他懷念住在她對面的那段日子。

opposite 可由 across from 取代，兩者意義相同。例如：

- The theme park is just **opposite / across from** our home.
  主題公園正好就在我們家對面。

from, to

Where do you come from?

I come from Australia.

How long will you stay here?

I'm just stopping over here for a couple of nights on the way to Beijing.

You're going to China. That's nice. There's a lot to see in Beijing. You'll love it.

英語介詞你要知

📣 介詞解讀與辨析

一般來説，from 指「從（某個地方）來」，to 指「往；向；朝（某個目的地、目標）去」。

⭐ 實用例句齊來學

from

- He comes **from** Sydney.
  他來自悉尼。

- Can you name a composer **from** China?
  你能說出一個來自中國的作曲家嗎？

- I got a parcel **from** my aunt yesterday.
  昨天我收到姨姨寄來的一個包裹。

to

- They went **to** the library.
  他們往圖書館去了。

- She goes **to** church every Sunday morning.
  她每個星期天早上都去教堂。

🔍 增潤知識大放送

from 和 to 經常連用，表達「從（某個地方）到（某個地方）」的意思。例如：

- The Island Line of the MTR runs **from** Kennedy Town **to** Chai Wan.
  港鐵港島線由堅尼地城行駛至柴灣。

- It takes ten minutes to go **from** the bus stop **to** the beach.
  由巴士站到海灘，需時十分鐘。

away from, towards

Something is flying towards me!

What's that?

Oh, it's a giant hornet! It looks fierce!

Watch out! It will sting you!

Oh, it's too late!

Run away from it! Run!

介詞解讀與辨析

away from 指某人或某物離開某一地方，到別的地方去。

towards 表示朝某人或某物的方向移動、看或指點。

away from 和 towards 的重點在於行動或動作的特定方向，而不是行動或動作的結果或者目標。

★ 實用例句齊來學

away from

- I walked **away from** a tree.
  我從樹下走開。

- They swam **away from** land.
  他們從陸地游出去了。

- She pulled **away from** him and jumped into the river.
  她掙脫開他，然後跳進河裏去。

towards

- A butterfly is flying **towards** me.
  一隻蝴蝶正向着我的方向飛來。

- The car is moving **towards** the cliff.
  汽車正朝着懸崖方向駛去。

- She looks back **towards** me.
  她回頭朝我看。

🔍 增潤知識大放送

在美式英語中，towards 會拼寫成 toward。

to 和 towards 有時可以互相替換來使用，但如果想強調向某具體方向移動，則用 towards 較好。例如：

- He stood up and walked **to / towards** me. 他站起身來，向我走來。

漫畫看一看

📢 介詞解讀與辨析

up 和 down 分別表示「由下而上」和「由上而下」兩個相反方向。

up 表示向上移動，例如上樓梯、爬梯子、上坡等。

down 表示向下移動，例如下樓梯、爬下梯子、沿着山坡往下走等。

★ 實用例句齊來學

up

- He is going **up** the stairs. 他正在上樓梯。
- The firefighter quickly climbed **up** the ladder and rescued the little boy. 那名消防員迅速爬上雲梯，把小男孩救了出來。

down

- Let's go **down** the slide. 我們從滑梯滑下去吧。
- The trolley was sliding **down** the slope. 手推車正從斜坡上滑下來。

🔍 增潤知識大放送

up 也可表示沿着道路行走，或向逆水而上的方向走。例如：

- She walked **up** the footpath slowly. 她沿着小徑緩慢向上走。
- They were sailing **up** the river. 他們往河的上游航行。

down 也可表示沿着道路往回走，或順着水流的方向走。例如：

- He walked back **down** the corridor. 他沿着走廊往回走。
- The raft floated **down** the stream. 木筏漂流而下。

俗語 be jumping up and down 指因生氣或興奮而蹦蹦跳跳。例如：

- The fans **were jumping up and down** and cheering.
  那些歌迷蹦跳歡呼。

漫畫看一看

介詞解讀與辨析

across 和 over 兩個介詞都是用來表示「從一邊到另一邊」的意思，主要涉及平面。

across 表示從一邊橫過到另一邊；over 表示從上面橫過、越過。

★ 實用例句齊來學

across

- The ferry is sailing **across** the harbour. 渡輪正在橫渡海港。

- An old man is slowly walking **across** the street.
  一位老人正在緩慢地走向街的對面。

- When we reached the river, we simply swam **across**.
  到河邊後，我們便直接游了過去。

over

- The children jumped **over** the fence. 那些孩子跳過了籬笆。

- The motorbike ran **over** the dog accidentally.
  那電單車意外地輾過了一隻狗。

- This car can travel **over** the most difficult ground.
  這汽車能在最難行的道路上行駛。

增潤知識大放送

across 和 over 都表示從一側移動到另一側，有時沒有明確的劃分，在一些上下文中，兩者甚至可以互相替代對方。例如：

- He drove **across** / **over** the bridge. 他開着汽車過橋。
- The ball rolled **across** / **over** the grass. 球滾過草地。

如果越過的是一個高的物體，就用 over（如：climb over the wall）；如果穿過的是一個平面，就用 across（如：wall across the street）。

漫畫看一看

🔨 介詞解讀與辨析

介詞 through 也是用來表示「從一邊到另一邊」的意思，既表示穿過或通過一端到另外一端，也指從兩旁的一羣事物或一堆物體中穿過，或指穿過某地區。

⭐ 實用例句齊來學

through

- The bus was passing **through** the tunnel.
  巴士在穿過隧道。

- Someone is peeping **through** the keyhole.
  有人透過鎖匙孔在偷窺。

- She pushed her way **through** the crowd to the door.
  她擠過人羣，來到門口。

- He drove straight **through** a red traffic light.
  他開車直闖紅燈。

- We passed **through** Nagoya on our way to Osaka.
  我們去大阪時途經名古屋。

🔍 增潤知識大放送

through 指「穿過」，所「穿過」的不一定是實物，也可以是不實在或抽象的東西。例如：

- I couldn't see **through** the mist.
  薄霧籠罩，我什麼也看不見。

- We all go **through** tough times.
  我們總會經歷艱難的日子。

漫畫看一看

Let's go this way. It's the fastest possible route.

No! I don't want to walk past the cemetery. That's scary!

All right. We can walk along the river to get to the destination. But that's a much longer route.

Don't worry. We have plenty of time. Let's go!

介詞解讀與辨析

along 和 past 用來表示不同的移動姿態。

along 解作「沿着」，例如沿着某物前進，如道路。

past 解作「經過」，例如從某人或某物旁邊經過。

along 和 past 的主要分別在於，前者後接一個可以遊走的路線，而後者後接一個擦身而過的點。

★ 實用例句齊來學

along

- The couple jogged **along** the seashore.
  一對夫婦沿着海邊慢跑。

- The drunkard failed to walk **along** a straight line.
  那醉漢不能沿着直線走。

past

- A car has just driven **past** me.
  一輛汽車剛剛從我身邊駛過。

- The murderer was last seen walking **past** the car park.
  有人見到謀殺犯在停車場走過，那是他最後一次露面。

增潤知識大放送

不要把介詞 past 和動詞 pass 混淆。例如我們不說：I saw Mary go passed the post office. 而說：I saw Mary go past the post office.（我看見瑪莉走過那郵局。）

動詞 pass 也指「經過」，但語法功能有所不同。例如：

- Mary **passed** the post office on her way back home.
  瑪莉回家途中經過那郵局。

get on, get into

漫畫看一看

介詞解讀與辨析

get on / get off 分別指「上車」、「下車」,用於可以在裏面站立的交通工具,例如巴士、火車、電車、輪船和飛機。除此之外,也可用於單車。

get in(to) / get out 也分別指「上車」、「下車」,用於只能坐在裏面的交通工具,例如汽車和的士。

實用例句齊來學

get on / get off

- We **got on** the bus and headed to the airport.
  我們乘搭巴士前往機場。

- She left her cell phone while **getting off** the train.
  她下火車時忘了帶手機。

- He **got on** his bicycle and rode off.
  他騎上單車走了。

get in(to) / get out

- I saw them **getting into** a red car.
  我看見他們坐上了一輛紅色的汽車。

- At the hotel, they **got out of** the taxi.
  他們在酒店下了的士。

增潤知識大放送

不要把「下車」說成 get down,例如我們不說:We got down the bus. 而說:We got off the bus.(我們下了巴士。)

📢 介詞解讀與辨析

「太陽從東邊升起」的「從」不能說成英語的 from，因為正確來說，地球繞着太陽轉，太陽升起的具體位置並不是東邊，因此要說 in the east（在東方）。但如果想要表達某人或某事「從」東邊過來，就可以用 from the east（從東方而來）。

⭐ 實用例句齊來學

in the east / south / west / north

- The landscape is more mountainous **in the south**. 南部多山。

from the east / south / west / north

- The wind blows **from the east** today. 今天風從東方吹來。

🔍 增潤知識大放送

to the east / south / west / north of 指「在……的東、南、西、北方」，例如：

- Cambridge lies **to the north of** London. 劍橋在倫敦北部。
- The airport is a few miles **to the west of** the city.
  機場位於城市以西數英里處。

towards the east / south / west / north 指「向東、南、西、北方而去」，例如：

- The army marched **towards the north**. 軍隊向北進發。

the East（E 字母作大寫）指「東方國家；亞洲國家」，例如：

- Martial arts originated in **the East**. 武術源自東方。

同樣地，the West（W 字母作大寫）則指「西方國家」，例如：

- He spent his childhood in **the West** — mostly in America.
  他在西方──主要是美國──度過了童年。

英語介詞你要知

介詞解讀與辨析

作為一個表達施行者關係的介詞，by 的意思是「被」，用於被動語態的動詞之後，解釋某人的動作或誰做了這個動作。by 後接施行者，這施行者可以是人、動物、機構或物體。

★ 實用例句齊來學

by

- The puppy was eaten **by** the crocodile.
  小狗被鱷魚吃掉。

- The blind man was led **by** the dog across the road.
  盲人被狗帶領過路。

- She was rasied **by** her grandparents.
  她由祖父母撫養成人。

- *Romeo and Juliet* was written **by** Shakespeare.
  《羅密歐與茱麗葉》由莎士比亞所著。

增潤知識大放送

跟隨在 by 後面的是動作的施行者，通常是有生命的個體，如上面例句的 crocodile、dog、grandparents、Shakespeare 等。

被動語態往往可以轉為主動語態，句中的施行者必須放回主動句中的主語位置，並刪掉介詞 by。例如：

- The **crocodile** ate the puppy. 鱷魚吃掉了小狗。

- The **dog** led the blind man across the road. 狗帶領盲人過路。

- Her **grandparents** rasied her. 她的祖父母把她撫養成人。

- **Shakespeare** wrote *Romeo and Juliet*.
  莎士比亞寫下《羅密歐與茱麗葉》。

漫畫看一看

Oh my goodness, what happened?

I don't know. When I got back, the house was already like that!

The sink was filled with water.

And the floor was covered with dirt. Everything was a mess!

Lucky, come on over! Is that you who made this terrible mess?

英語介詞你要知 ✏️

🔍 介詞解讀與辨析

在被動語態句子中，雖然施行者往往是由 by 帶出，但在少數及物動詞句子中，也會用上 with。

作為一個表達施行者關係的介詞，with 的意思同樣是「被」，用於被動語態的動詞之後，解釋了執行該動作所使用的東西、某人行動時的狀態或誰做了這個動作。

⭐ 實用例句齊來學

with

- The bathtub is filled **with** water. 浴缸裝滿了水。
- The slope is covered **with** snow. 斜坡上覆蓋着雪。
- Little Tom is overcome **with** fear. 小湯姆恐懼不已。
- Her room is decorated **with** small paintings. 她的房間有小畫裝飾。
- During the World Cup, the streets were filled **with** football fans. 世界盃比賽期間，街上擠滿了球迷。

🔍 增潤知識大放送

在被動語態的結構裏，介詞 with 連接了動作的承受者（如以上例句的 bathtub、slope、Little Tom 等）和施行者（如以上例句的 water、snow、fear 等）。

但仔細研究以上例句，會發現每一個介詞 with 的賓語都不是有生命的個體，例如真正把浴缸裝滿的施行者不是水，而是在句子中沒有提到的人。相比之下，by 在被動語態句子中作為表達施行者關係介詞的角色，就明顯得多了。

漫畫看一看

📢 介詞解讀與辨析

作為施行者介詞，about 用來表示某人的言語、思想或情感與某事有關。about 指「有關；關於；在⋯⋯方面」。它可用在動詞 be 或其他動詞之後，也可用在名詞或形容詞後。

⭐ 實用例句齊來學

about

- The film is **about** the love between a mermaid and a prince.
  那電影講述美人魚和王子之間的愛情。

- We were talking **about** UFOs.
  我們當時正談論不明飛行物。

- She cares very much **about** her appearance.
  她很在意自己的外表。

- This is a magazine **about** fishing.
  這是一本關於釣魚的雜誌。

- That comic **about** wildlife animals is very interesting.
  那本關於野生動物的漫畫很有趣。

- We are so worried **about** you.
  我們非常擔心你。

- The passengers were very angry **about** the flight delay.
  乘客對航班延誤感到十分生氣。

🔍 增潤知識大放送

about 有時可用於會話中，帶出說話者所要談到的內容。例如：

- **About** the school trip tomorrow, please make sure you arrive at the meeting point at least fifteen minutes early.
  至於明天的學校旅行，請務必提早至少十五分鐘到達集合點。

漫畫看一看

It's great seeing you today.

You too.

No. I'll go back on foot. I live nearby.

METRO

BUS

So, where are you heading? Shall we go by metro or by bus?

Alright. Let's keep in touch.

Yeap, of course.

You can always contact me by telephone or by email.

Sure.

介詞解讀與辨析

作為一個表示工具的介詞，by 指「靠⋯⋯；由⋯⋯；用⋯⋯」，表示藉着用某種方式做某事，或乘搭某種交通工具或使用某種運輸途徑。

實用例句齊來學

by

- We sometimes communicate with our teachers **by** email.
  我們有時會用電郵和老師溝通。

- We can now obtain the latest news **by** various means.
  我們現在可以通過各種途徑獲得最新消息。

- Lily learnt English **by** listening to English songs.
  莉莉透過聽英文歌曲來學習英語。

- She comes home **by** bus.
  她坐巴士回家。

- Shall we go **by** MTR?
  我們要坐港鐵去嗎？

- How much is it to send this parcel **by** sea?
  由海路寄送這個包裹要多少錢？

增潤知識大放送

用於乘搭交通工具的介詞主要是 by，但如果選擇步行，介詞需用 on，而介詞短語則是 on foot。例如：

- She goes to school **on foot**.
  她步行上學。

- Are you going by bus or **on foot**?
  你坐巴士去還是走路去？

漫畫看一看

We're going to make a dragon today.

First, colour the drawing **with** crayons.

Then, cut the shapes out **with** a pair of scissors.

Now, join the pieces **with** glue. And...look! It's done!

介詞解讀與辨析

作為一個表示工具的介詞，with 的意思是「以……；用……」，
後接某種工具、材料或物體來完成某事。

實用例句齊來學

with

- Wipe your mouth **with** a tissue. 用紙巾擦嘴巴。

- She opened the walnuts **with** a hammer. 她用錘子打開核桃。

- Mix the flour **with** butter. 把麵粉和牛油混和在一起。

- The carpenter makes all furniture **with** wood.
  木匠以木材製造所有家具。

- She feeds the plants twice a month **with** fertilisers.
  她一個月兩次為植物施肥。

- Cats love cleaning their front paws **with** their tongue.
  貓喜歡用牠們的舌頭清潔前爪。

增潤知識大放送

緊接 with 後面的也可以是手段或比較抽象的概念。例如：

- Don't solve problems **with** violence.
  不要以暴力解決問題。

- She won the debate **with** her eloquence.
  她以口才贏了辯論。

with 的反義詞是 without，意指「沒有、無」。例如：

- I can't catch fish **without** a net.
  沒有網，我無法捕魚。

- She couldn't join the pieces together **without** glue.
  沒有膠水，她無法把這兩塊黏在一起。

漫畫看一看

介詞解讀與辨析

作為表示比較的介詞，as 和 like 的意思是「如同；像」，後接名詞或名詞短語。

as 指「像……一樣，如同；作為，以……身分」。

like 指「像；與……相似」。

實用例句齊來學

as

- I'm going to the fancy dress party **as** Doraemon.
  我會裝扮成哆啦 A 夢一樣去參加化妝舞會。

- The hospital ward is decorated **as** a hotel room.
  醫院病房裝飾得像酒店房間。

like

- He was dressed **like** a prince. 他穿戴得像個王子。

- She lives life **like** a princess. 她過着如同公主般的生活。

增潤知識大放送

道理上，as 和 like 可以交換使用，但從實際的語義上來看，as 與 like 作介詞用時還是有一點差別。as 這個「像」，它的相像程度較高一些，所以我們一般都譯作「作為」；而 like 這個「像」就是單純的「像」，它沒有「像」到「是」那個地步。例如：

- She speaks English **as** a British.
- She speaks English **like** a British.

以上兩句雖然都表示她説英語像英國人，但程度是不一樣的。用 as 的句子表示和真正的英國人沒什麼差別，而用 like 的句子就僅僅是像而已。

漫畫看一看

We want the school to ban all exams. Do you vote for or against this proposal?

I vote for it because exams cause a lot of stress and anxiety.

I am against it!

Why?

It's because exams can consolidate learning and push us to study.

What about the rest of you? Let's vote!

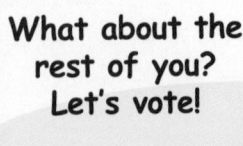

介詞解讀與辨析

against 用來對比兩件事物的差異,帶有「對照;對比」的意思。它可表示「反對;與……相反」,也可指「和……對照;以……作襯托」。

實用例句齊來學

against

- A hundred people voted **against** the proposal.
  一百人投票反對這項新提案。

- The dark colour of the shirt looks odd **against** your fair skin.
  對比你白皙的皮膚,深色的襯衫看起來很奇怪。

- She showed off the ten medals she's won at school, **against** the two I have.
  她炫耀在學校贏得的十枚獎牌,比對我有的兩枚。

- The government often has to weigh the pros **against** the cons of different proposals.
  政府經常要權衡不同提案的利弊輕重。

增潤知識大放送

against 的反義詞是 for,解作「贊成;支持」。例如:

- I'll never vote **for** him again. 我決不再投他的票。

慣用語 against the law / rules 指「違法 / 違章」。例如:

- It's **against the law** to drive too fast. 超速駕駛是違法的。

慣用語 have something against someone 指「因(某種原因)不喜歡(某人)」。例如:

- I **have nothing against** you. 我一點都不討厭你。

漫畫看一看

How was your weekend?

We went camping in spite the rain.

Did you mean that in spite of the rain, you guys still went camping?

Yes. Thanks for correcting my mistake.

Got it! Thanks, mum.

You may also say "Despite the rain, we went camping."

📢 介詞解讀與辨析

in spite of 和 despite 的意思相同，中文解作「儘管；雖然」，表示兩件事物之間的轉折關係。兩者可以交換使用，但要記住，in spite of 是三個字，且一定要有 of，而 despite 後面不可有 of。除此之外，兩者後面必須搭配名詞或動名詞 (gerund)。

⭐ 實用例句齊來學

in spite of

- **In spite of** the rain, we went hiking.
  雖然天下着雨，我們還是去了遠足。
- She still liked him **in spite of** the way he behaved.
  儘管他有那樣的所作所為，她還是愛他。

despite

- **Despite** the bad weather, we still enjoyed our holiday.
  儘管天氣不好，我們依然享受我們的假期。
- We enjoyed the rides **despite** the long queues.
  儘管很多人排隊，我們還是很享受這些遊樂設施。

🔍 增潤知識大放送

in spite of 和 despite 通常用在英文寫作，比較少用於口語。而 despite 比 in spite of 略微正式。

in spite of 和 despite 後面不能接句子，如要接句子必須加上 the fact that。例如：

- It was very hot **in spite of / despite the fact that** it was only the end of April.
  儘管才四月底，天氣已經很熱了。

for all, with all

漫畫看一看

Sometimes he's very rude!

Sometimes he's careless!

Sometimes he's impatient with others!

Sometimes he talks too much!

But for all his weaknesses, he's still a really good friend.

Yes. With all his faults, we still like him.

介詞解讀與辨析

在 for all 或 with all 的結構中，for 和 with 是介詞，all 作後面的名詞片語的修飾語；for all 或 with all 表示對立和讓步，一般翻譯為「儘管；雖然」。

for all 或 with all 放於句首，後接名詞片語，與餘下的主句 (main clause) 產生強烈的對比，以突顯其與主句的對立和讓步的幅度。

★ 實用例句齊來學

For all

- **For all** her efforts, she didn't succeed.
  她雖然很努力，但她沒有成功。

- **For all** the nice talk, I don't trust him.
  儘管他說話漂亮，但我不信任他。

- **For all** her weaknesses, she has always been a very good friend.
  儘管她有很多弱點，但她一直是很好的朋友。

With all

- **With all** his money, Uncle Sam isn't happy.
  山姆叔叔儘管很有錢，但他不開心。

- **With all** her achievements, she never boasts.
  儘管她很有成就，但她從不自誇。

增潤知識大放送

for all 或 with all 可由 despite 或 in spite of 取代。例如：

- **For all / With all / Despite / In spite of** his qualifications, he still couldn't find a job.
  儘管他具有資歷，但他仍找不到工作。

漫畫看一看

What is the colour of its fur?

Well, it tends to be yellow gold.

Is it a member of the cat family?

Does it have a mane?

Yes, it is.

Yes, it does.

I know. It's Lion King, the king of the forest!

Bingo!

介詞解讀與辨析

英語中表示組成部分的介詞只有 of 一個，它是使用頻率最高的介詞，用於各式各樣的場合。

of 解作「……的；屬於……」，表示事物或事情的某一部分。事物的部分往往放在 of 前面，事物的整體則放在後面。

實用例句齊來學

of

- What's the name **of** that insect? 那隻昆蟲的名字是什麼？

- I don't like the smell **of** the paint. 我不喜歡油漆的氣味。

- This clock tower is the property **of** the government.
  這座鐘樓是屬於政府的財產。

- Memories **of** the past keep haunting her.
  屬於過去的回憶一直困擾着她。

增潤知識大放送

使用表示組成部分的介詞 of 時，部分和整體的出場次序在中英文剛好相反。例如，「油漆的氣味」會説成 the smell of the paint，而不是 the paint of the smell；「屬於過去的回憶」會説成 memories of the past，而不是 the past of memories。

如果後接 of 的是人物，那麼使用所有格形容詞 (possessive adjective) 或者所有格的名詞短語 (possessive noun phrase) 來表達，意思會更簡單利落。例如：

- What's **his** name? 他的名字是什麼？

如果後接 of 的不是人或賦予生命的個體，還是選用 of 比較穩妥。例如：

- What's the name **of** that tower? 那座塔的名字是什麼？

漫畫看一看

介詞解讀與辨析

plus 是「加;加上」,提及要增加的內容或數量時,一般放在要被加起的兩個數值之間。

minus 是「減;減去」,一般放在要被減去的原先數值之後和要拿掉的數額之前。

★ 實用例句齊來學

plus

- One **plus** two equals three. 一加二等於三。
- The buffet costs each of us $498 **plus** 10% service charge. 自助餐的消費是每位 498 元,外加百分之十的服務費。

minus

- Three **minus** two equals one. 三減二等於一。
- The selling price **minus** the cost is the profit. 售價減去成本就是利潤。

增潤知識大放送

注意 plus 和 minus 的拼寫,都是以 s 結尾,這個 s 字母不能刪去,不能寫成 plu 和 minu。

透過 plus 或 minus 來增加或減掉的東西,可以是事物或抽象概念。例如:

- What you need to succeed is diligence **plus** some luck. 成功需苦幹,還要一點運氣。
- My uncle looks exactly alike my dad **minus** the thick glasses. 我爸爸把厚厚的眼鏡除下後,樣子跟我叔叔一模一樣。

表達算式時,plus 可換成連接詞 and,同樣後接單數動詞。例如:

- Five **and** five equals ten. 五加五等於十。

times, by

漫畫看一看

介詞解讀與辨析

介詞 times 指「乘」，一般放在兩個數值之間。

介詞 by 只要配搭動詞 divide，便可以帶出「除」的意思。

★ 實用例句齊來學

times

- Three **times** six is eighteen.
  三乘六是十八。

- Five **times** five equals twenty-five.
  五乘五等於二十五。

(divide) by

- **Divide** eighteen **by** six and you get three. / Eighteen **divided by** six equals three. 十八除六得三。

- **Divide** six **by** three to get two. / Six **divided by** three to get two. 六除二得三。

增潤知識大放送

要表達「乘」的意思，by 亦是另一個可表示計算的介詞，但它需要與動詞 multiply 連用。例如：

- **Multiply** two **by** three and you get six.
  二乘三得六。

- **Multiply** three **by** six to get eighteen.
  三乘六得十八。

注意 times 的拼寫，必須有 s，不能寫作 time。例如：

- Two **times** three equals six.
  二乘三得六。

漫畫看一看

These apples look good and fresh!

Let's buy some. Our children love apples.

We can buy them singly or by the dozen. What do you think?

If we buy them singly, it is $5 each.

🍎 = $5

= $48

If we buy them by the dozen, it's $4 per apple.

Okay. Let's buy a dozen.

$4

$4

$4

、介詞解讀與辨析

by 與 per 是兩個與計算單位關係密切的介詞，一般放在某計算單位之前。

by 是「按；以……計」的意思。

per 是「每」的意思，表示速度或比率。

★ 實用例句齊來學

by

- You will get paid **by** the hour. 你的工資將按小時支付。

- Visitors come through the border **by** the thousand.
  數以千計的遊客通過邊境前來。

per

- There are roughly thirty pupils **per** class. 每班大約有三十個學生。

- On average, how much do you spend **per** day?
  平均而言，你每天花多少錢？

- How many public holidays are there in Hong Kong **per** year?
  香港每年有多少公眾假期呢？

○ 增潤知識大放送

在表示計算的介詞 by 後面的名詞短語，通常用 the 來開始。
例如：by the hour、by the pound、by the dozen。

使用介詞 per 來表示計算單位的常見片語，有時會以縮寫甚至符號形式出現。例如：

- **per** annum → p.a. 每年

- miles **per** hour → m.p.h. 每小時……英里

- **per** cent → % 百分之……

漫畫看一看

Here are the survey results, sir. Half of the students in our class wear glasses.

A quarter of them don't like sports.

And two out of three girls don't do any sports in the past year.

Among the boys, four out of ten are overweight.

SPORTS DAY

No way! We have to do something about this.

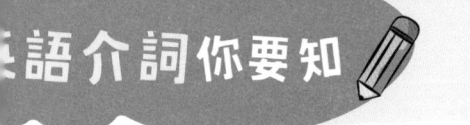 

英語介詞你要知

介詞解讀與辨析

of 和 out of 這兩個介詞都可以用作計算或統計某事物。

of 用來表達「⋯⋯之中的」的意思。

out of 用來表示所談論的事物的比例。

實用例句齊來學

of

• He knows only a quarter **of** the classmates by name.
  他知道只有四分之一同學的名字。

• I need half a pound **of** cheese.
  我需要半磅芝士。

• Dad brought home five gallons **of** petrol.
  爸爸帶了五加侖汽油回家。

out of

• Three **out of** five users choose this smartphone.
  五個用家之中就有三人選用這部智能電話。

• Within this age range, four **out of** ten were unemployed.
  在這個年齡組別裏，十人中有四人失業。

• No one got fifty **out of** fifty in the quiz competition.
  這次問答比賽，沒有人答對全部五十道題。

增潤知識大放送

以上兩個表示計算或統計的介詞大多涉及基數 (cardinal numbers)，數值放在介詞之前。例如：

• one litre **of** orange juice 一升橙汁

• three **out of** ten girls 十分之三的女孩

漫畫看一看

You're late! I've been waiting for you for an hour.

I'm so sorry. My motorbike broke down in the middle of nowhere...

...and I've to walk for miles to get here.

Here's some food for you. Forgive me, please.

Wow!

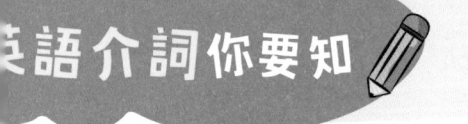

📣 介詞解讀與辨析

for 既可用來表示持續的時間，也可用來表示延續的距離或其他計算單位，具有「達」或「計」的意思。

⭐ 實用例句齊來學

for

- I've been waiting here **for** two hours.
  我一直在這裏等了兩個小時。

- She's going on a trip **for** three days.
  她要出門旅遊三天。

- They've been driving **for** a hundred miles.
  他們已行駛一百英里。

- He sold his old watch **for** five thousand bucks.
  他以五千元賣掉了自己的舊手錶。

🔍 增潤知識大放送

表示計算的介詞 for 大多涉及基數 (cardinal numbers)，數值需放在介詞之後。例如：

- He reads **for** two hours each night.
  他每晚閱讀兩個小時。

如不能確定實際的時間或距離，可不用基數。例如：

- I haven't played the piano **for** years.
  我已好多年沒彈鋼琴了。

- We ran **for** miles.
  我們跑了數英里。

- Because of the typhoon, we've been stuck in this hotel **for** days.
  由於颱風來襲，我們被困在這家酒店好幾天了。

because of

漫畫看一看

I'm afraid we won't be able to go to see you this weekend.

Why?

We can't fly. The airport is closed because of the heavy snow.

And our flight is cancelled because of the bad weather.

That's too bad. Anyway, safety first. We'll see each other soon.

You're right.

📣 介詞解讀與辨析

because of 指「因為；由於」，是短語介詞，用來表示原因，一般放在原因之前。如放於句首，可起強調作用。

⭐ 實用例句齊來學

because of

- Parents make lots of sacrifice for their kids **because of** love.
  因為愛，父母為自己的孩子作出很多犧牲。

- He has regained self-confidence **because of** your encouragement. 因為你的鼓勵，他已經恢復自信。

- **Because of** the poor service, the restaurant has been blacklisted. 由於服務質素差，該餐廳已被列入黑名單。

🔍 增潤知識大放送

雖然 because 和 because of 一般都被譯成「因為；由於」，但是前者後接子句，是連接詞，而後者接名詞短語，是介詞。例如：

- He seldom dines out **because** his income is low.
  他很少外出用膳，因為他收入微薄。

- He seldom dines out **because of** his low income.
  他很少外出用膳，因為他收入微薄。

留意 because 始終是連接詞，顧名思義，是應該用來連接句子中間的組成部分。故此，應盡量不要把它放在句子開端。

而 because of 是介詞，只要後接名詞短語形成介詞短語，便沒有 because 在句子中位置上的禁忌，如放在句子開頭，可起強調作用。例如：

- **Because of** his low income, he seldom dines out.
  因為他收入微薄，他很少外出用膳。

漫畫看一看

介詞解讀與辨析

跟 because of 一樣，due to、owing to 和 thanks to 都是表示原因的短語介詞，三者都指「由於；因為」，可以隨意互換使用。

實用例句齊來學

due to

- The train was delayed **due to** the heavy snow.
  火車因為大雪延誤了。

owing to

- The picnic has been cancelled **owing to** the bad weather.
  由於天氣惡劣，野餐取消了。

thanks to

- Grandma is slowly recovering **thanks to** your help.
  感謝你的幫忙，祖母正在慢慢康復過來。

增潤知識大放送

due to、owing to 和 thanks to 後接表示原因的名詞或名詞短語，不能接句子。

因為 thanks to 有「幸虧；多得」的意思，所以後面也可接人物。例如：

- It's **thanks to** Lily that I found my lost cellphone.
  幸虧莉莉，我才找回遺失了的手機。

使用 owing to 和 thanks to 時要注意拼寫，是 owing，而不是 owning；是 thanks，而不是 thank。例如：

- **Owing to** the accident, she broke her right leg.
  因為出了意外，她的右腿給摔斷了。

漫畫看一看

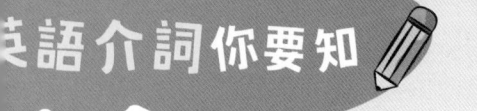

介詞解讀與辨析

英語中表示目的的介詞最主要是 for。for 既可指「為了（某目的）」，也可表達「為了要；為了獲得」的意思。

★ 實用例句齊來學

for

- This exit is **for** emergency only.
  此出口僅作緊急用途。

- The washrooms in this restaurant are **for** eat-in customers only.
  這家餐廳的洗手間只供食客使用。

- She went to the supermarket **for** some milk.
  她去超級市場買了一些牛奶。

- Dad is applying **for** the post of Senior Lecturer.
  爸爸正在申請高級講師的職位。

- Your mum is there, waiting **for** you.
  你媽媽在那兒等着你。

- **For** further information, please contact our manager.
  如欲了解更多資訊，請聯絡我們的經理。

增潤知識大放送

for 作為表示目的的介詞時，後面必須接名詞或名詞短語。

for 也可作連接詞用，意指「因為；由於」，後接子句。比較以下句子：

- [介詞] She went to the bakery **for** some bread.
  她去麵包店買了一些麵包。

- [連接詞] She went to the bakery **for** she needed some bread.
  她去麵包店，因為她要買麵包。

漫畫看一看

You're trembling with fear, aren't you? What's the matter?

With exams coming, I just feel so nervous.

SILENCE
EXAM IN PROGRESS

Take it easy! Don't worry too much.

Do you have any advice for me?

Last time, through hard work, I passed all the exams. I believe you can, too.

Thank you.

英語介詞你要知

📢 介詞解讀與辨析

介詞 through 和 with 都有「因為；由於」的意思，可以用來帶出某些原因。

⭐ 實用例句齊來學

through

- I met Jessica **through** John.
  我通過約翰認識了潔西嘉。

- A lot of water is wasted **through** leakage.
  由於洩漏，大量水給浪費掉了。

- The refugees fled their village **through** fear.
  那些難民因為恐懼而逃離了鄉村。

with

- We laughed **with** joy. 我們高興得放聲大笑。

- Mum has been at home **with** a bad cold.
  媽媽因患了重感冒一直在家休息。

- The buffet wasn't cheap **with** the service charge.
  由於要收取服務費，那自助餐並不便宜。

🔍 增潤知識大放送

through 和 with 可以放在句子開頭，以起強調作用。當把解釋原因的部分放在句子開端時，後面需要加上逗號來連接主要子句，例如：

- **Through** hard work, Wayne got straight As in all the subjects.
  通過努力，韋恩所有科目都取得甲等成績。

- **With** exams coming, we are feeling increasingly stressed.
  由於考試快到，我們壓力越來越大。

介詞解讀與辨析

我們經常用介詞 with 來表達某種做事的方式。with 後接人物時，表示「和、同」，即是與某人在一起。除此之外，with 也可表達某人做事時的行為、方式。

★ 實用例句齊來學

with

- Jenny likes going shopping **with** her mum.
  珍妮喜歡和媽媽一起去購物。

- Anne enjoys walking hand in hand **with** her elder sister.
  安妮喜歡跟姊姊手牽手漫步。

- The two boys are fishing **with** their dad at the pier.
  兩個男孩與他們的父親在碼頭釣魚。

- She finished her work **with** great accuracy.
  她極其準確地完成了工作。

- He ate **with** great difficulty.
  他吞嚥十分困難。

- She spoke **with** an American accent.
  她說話帶有美國口音。

增潤知識大放送

表示方式的介詞 with 和表示工具的介詞 with 最大的分別是，它們分別後接什麼。前者一般後接人或賦予生命的個體，而後者一般是工具、本身沒有生命的東西或比較抽象的概念。例如：

- [表示方式的 **with**] They live **with** their grandparents.
  他們和祖父母一起居住。

- [表示工具的 **with**] He hit the nail **with** a hammer.
  他用錘子敲釘子。

漫畫看一看

🔊 介詞解讀與辨析

in 指經歷某種狀態或處境，並受其影響；或指說話或寫作等的方式。

⭐ 實用例句齊來學

in

- I am **in** pain! 我很痛！

- They are not **in** danger. 他們沒有危險。

- Have you ever been **in** love? 你談過戀愛嗎？

- The ceremony finished **in** good order.
  儀式在良好的秩序中結束。

- They spoke **in** Shanghainese the whole time.
  他們一直用上海話交談。

- The email was **in** Japanese.
  這封電郵是用日語寫的。

- The patient speaks **in** a very low voice.
  這病人說話時聲音低沉。

- He likes to paint **in** watercolour.
  他喜歡用水彩畫畫。

🔍 增潤知識大放送

表示方式的介詞 in 和表示時間或位置的介詞 in 的最大分別之處，在於它們分別後接什麼。前者一般後接表示「狀態」的內容，而後者後接的都是時間或空間。例如：

- [表示方式的 **in**] We're **in** a hurry. 我們很着急。

- [表示位置的 **in**] We live **in** Hong Kong. 我們住在香港。

漫畫看一看

I saw Lily today. She came to the party with a pink dress.

Why's that?

Did she go shopping before the party?

Did she buy a new dress?

Oh, no! I mean she came to the party in a pink dress.

I see. She always looks nice in pink.

Yes. Pink suits her very well.

介詞解讀與辨析

介詞 in 和 with 在不同情景中有不同意思。

in 的其中一個意思是「穿着；穿戴」。

而 with 則用來表示擁有某物或某特徵，例如指出某人所攜帶的物品，或用來描述某人的外形特徵。

實用例句齊來學

in

- Who was the girl **in** the yellow dress?
  那個穿黃色裙子的女孩是誰？

- Fred looks very handsome **in** his uniform.
  費雷德穿着制服看起來很英俊。

- Between the trees I caught sight of a woman **in** black trousers.
  在樹林間，我看到了一個穿黑褲子的女人。

with

- I saw a man **with** a cut on his face.
  我見到一個臉上有傷痕的男人。

- They were talking to a woman **with** a large basket.
  他們當時正和手提大籃子的女子談話。

- That tall man **with** dark hair speaks with a foreign accent.
  那個黑髮的高個子男人說話時有外國口音。

增潤知識大放送

in 可以用來表示人所穿的衣服，在後面直接加顏色，就能表示穿了什麼顏色的衣服。例如：

- You look nice **in** blue.
  你穿藍色衣服很好看。

agree, agree to, agree with, agree on

介詞解讀與辨析

agree 解作「同意；贊同」，多作不及物動詞用。

若同意的是一件事，agree 後必須接介詞 to。

若同意的對象是人，即同意某人的看法，agree 後必須接介詞 with。

若雙方或多方就某事達成協議，表示一致同意，則用 agree on。

實用例句齊來學

agree

• John and I rarely **agree**.
我和約翰意見很少一致。

agree to something

• We would never **agree to** such a plan.
我們絕對不會贊成這樣一個計劃。

agree with someone

• All of them **agreed with** me on this issue.
在這個議題上，他們所有人都贊同我的意見。

agree on something

• We couldn't **agree on** which ice cream to buy.
我們無法就買哪一種冰淇淋達成一致意見。

增潤知識大放送

agree 可接 that-clause 或 to do something，例如：

• We all **agreed that** Linda should be invited.
我們都同意邀請琳達來。

• They **agreed to meet** again soon.
他們同意很快再見面。

漫畫看一看

Why are you crying?

My two dogs died.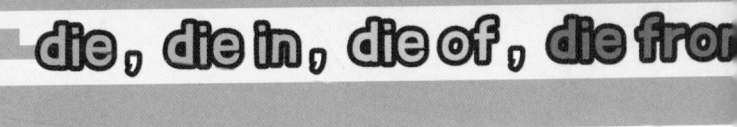

Why? What happened to them?

Lucky died in his sleep. He died of old age.

Susie refused to eat for ten days. She died from hunger.

Sorry to hear about this. Don't be sad. Heaven is filled with love, so Lucky and Susie should feel right at home there.

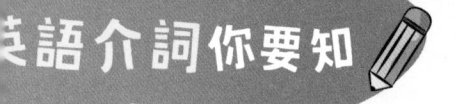  

介詞解讀與辨析

die 解作「死亡；消逝」，作不及物動詞用。

die in 後接火災、車禍等意外的死因。

die of 後接從身體內部引發的死因，如疾病、年老等。

die from 後接外在因素引起的死因。

★ 實用例句齊來學

die

- Ten people **died**. 有十人喪生。
- Our love will never **die**. 我們的愛永不消逝。

die in

- The old man **died in** a house fire. 那老人死於一場火災。
- She **died** peacefully **in** her sleep. 她在睡眠中安然辭世。
- Three people **died in** the car accident last week.
  上周的車禍中有三人死亡。

die of

- The old man **died of** lung cancer. 那老人死於肺癌。
- They say she **died of** a broken heart. 他們說她因為傷心過度而死。

die from

- He **died from** multiple gunshot wounds. 他死於多處槍傷。
- Some refugees **died from** hunger. 有些難民餓死了。

增潤知識大放送

die of 和 die from 有時很難區分，以下兩種場合經常互相使用，
例如：

- He **died of** / **died from** a heart attack. 他死於心臟病發作。
- These animals **died of** / **died from** starvation. 這些動物餓死了。

漫畫看一看

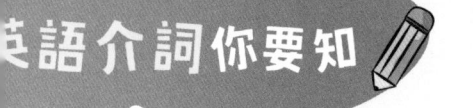  

英語介詞你要知

📢 介詞解讀與辨析

fill 解作「填塞；裝滿；充滿」，多作及物動詞用。

fill 加上介詞 in 解作「填寫」，通常是填寫正式文件或表格。

fill 加上介詞 up 則解作「填滿」。

fill 和 fill up 都有「填滿」的意思，fill up 特別強調把某容器裝滿到頂。

★ 實用例句齊來學

fill

- **Fill** the glass with water. 把杯子盛滿水。

- He **filled** most of his time playing with his phone.
  他靠着玩手機打發大部分時間。

fill in

- Please **fill in** the application form. 請填寫申請表格。

- **Fill in** the answers to these questions. 填寫這些問題的答案。

fill up

- He **filled up** the bowl with hot water. 他在碗裏加滿了熱水。

- Her eyes **filled up** with tears. 她眼中充滿了淚水。

🔍 增潤知識大放送

fill in 也可由 fill out 替代。例如：

- Would you mind **filling out** this questionnaire for me?
  你可以幫我填寫這份問卷嗎？

我們不能說 fill a form / questionnaire，而說 fill in / out a form / questionnaire，當中的介詞 in 或 out 不能刪去。

fill up 也可指「吃飽」，一般用於口語中。例如：

- Don't **fill** yourself **up** with snacks. 別吃太多零食。

漫畫看一看

What are your strengths and weaknesses?

I'm never good at sports.

But I'm good at languages. I'm good with people, too.

안녕하세요.

你 好。

Hello.

Bonjour.

Good!

If given a chance, I'll do my best for the success of your company!

That's great! Can you come to work next Monday?

英語介詞你要知

📢 介詞解讀與辨析

good at 和 good with 兩個片語意思接近，good 都有「好；擅長」的意思，區別就在介詞 at 和 with。

good at 強調「擅長於（某事）」，其賓語往往指「技能、學科、體育運動等」之類的詞語。

good with 強調「擅長對待……；擅長和……相處」，其賓語一般是人，有時也可以跟具體的事物。

⭐ 實用例句齊來學

good at something / doing something

- John is **good at** maths. 約翰擅長數學。
- Sarah is **good at** badminton. 莎拉擅長打羽毛球。
- I am not **good at** singing. 我不會唱歌。

good with someone / something

- She is very **good with** people. 她很會和人打交道。
- He is very **good with** children, looking after them very well. 他很擅長和小孩相處，把他們照顧得很好。
- Lily is very **good with** words. 莉莉善於辭令。

🔍 增潤知識大放送

good at 的反義詞是 bad at。例如：

- She is very **bad at** cooking. 她的廚藝很差。

good / bad at something 中的 at 不能由 in 取代，例如我們不說：Tom is good in making things. 而說：Tom is good at making things.（湯姆很會做東西。）

漫畫看一看

Why are you interested in writing comics?

I find your books very interesting indeed. Can you tell us something about your new comic?

I think comics are great for telling stories.

My new comic book is about aliens and UFOs.

That's great. I'd be very interested to read it as soon as possible.

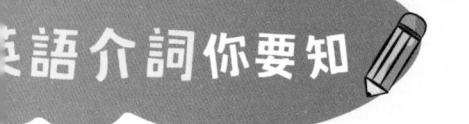

英語介詞你要知

📢 介詞解讀與辨析

形容詞 interested 解作「感興趣的」。

interested 後接介詞 in something / doing something 時，表示「對……感興趣」。

interested 後接介詞 to do something 時，表示「很想……」。

⭐ 實用例句齊來學

interested

- I've got a spare ticket for the concert if you're **interested**.
  如果你感興趣，我這裏多了一張演唱會門票。

interested in something / doing something

- He's always been **interested in** music.
  他一直對音樂感興趣。

- I'm **interested in** reading novels.
  我對閱讀小說感興趣。

interested to do something

- I'd be very **interested to** hear your story.
  我非常想聽聽你的故事。

- We'd be **interested to** know what you think about the plan.
  我們很想知道你對這計劃的想法。

🔍 增潤知識大放送

不要混淆 interested 和 interesting。interested 指一種感受，句子的主語應該是人，interesting 指某事使你感興趣，句子的主語不一定是人。例如：

- Anna is **interested in** ballet. 安娜對芭蕾舞感興趣。

- This book is **interesting**. 這本書很有趣。

119

made of , made from

漫畫看一看

Teacher Panda, how are books made?

Most books are made of paper.

But where does paper come from?

Paper comes from trees! In fact, most of the paper we use today is made from trees!

英語介詞你要知

⚡ 介詞解讀與辨析

made of 指「由……製成」，通常用來談論某事物的基本原料或元素，而在製作過程中，這些原料本質不變。

made from 也指「由……製成」，通常用於表達某事物是被加工製造的，在製作過程中，完全改變了原料本質。

★ 實用例句齊來學

made of

- This table is **made of** wood. 這張桌子是由木頭製成的。
- She wore a beautiful bracelet **made of** gold.
  她戴着一條漂亮的金手鐲。

made from

- Wine is **made from** grapes. 紅酒是由葡萄製造而成的。
- Plastic is **made from** oil. 塑膠是由石油製成的。
- Bread is **made from** flour. 麵包是由麵粉製成的。

🔍 增潤知識大放送

慣用語 be made of money 指「（人）十分富有」，例如：

- I'm not buying you another PC. I'm not **made of money**!
  我不會再給你買電腦，我又不是很有錢！

在談論食品和飲料中的成分時，我們常說 be made with，而不說 be made of。例如：

- Sushi **is made with** raw fish. 壽司用魚生做的。

假如某件物品的用途被改變了，我們就可以使用 be made out of。例如：

- These bricks **are made out of** cigarette butts.
  這些磚頭是用煙頭做的。

prefer to , rather than

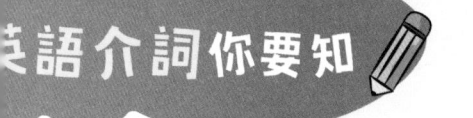

介詞解讀與辨析

介詞短語 prefer to 和 rather than 都是用來比較兩件事物或兩個動作，意思是「寧可；寧願；更喜歡……」，用來強調「偏好」。

prefer A to B 的意思是「比起 A，更喜歡 B」。

而 A rather than B 的意思則是「A 而不是 B」。

★ 實用例句齊來學

prefer A to B

- I **prefer** white **to** black. 比起黑色，我更喜歡白色。
- She **prefers** swimming **to** playing basketball.
  比起打籃球，她更喜歡游泳。

A rather than B

- I like to eat chocolate cakes **rather than** lemon cakes.
  我喜歡吃巧克力蛋糕，而不是檸檬蛋糕。
- **Rather than** taking a school bus, I go to school on foot.
  我走路上學，而不是坐校巴上學。

增潤知識大放送

必須注意的是，prefer A to B 是固定搭配，不可使用 than 來替代介詞 to。例如我們不說：Dad prefers coffee than tea. 而說：Dad prefers coffee to tea.（相比喝茶，爸爸更喜歡喝咖啡。）

如用於問題，讓對方作出選擇時，則可說成 prefer A or B。例如：

- Do you **prefer** coffee **or** tea? 你喜歡咖啡還是茶？

A rather than B 也是固定搭配，例如我們不說：I'll have tea rather to coffee. 而說：I'll have tea rather than coffee.（我要茶，不要咖啡。）

漫畫看一看

What's your dream?

My dream is to be an astronaut.

Why?

I want to go to space. Some day, I want to reach Mars!

Is it possible?

Why not? My parents always encourage me to reach for the stars!

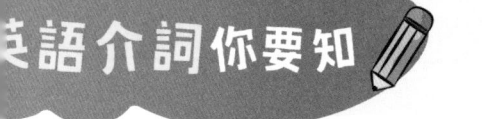  
介詞解讀與辨析

reach 有多重意義，它可解作「到達；抵達」，作及物動詞用，後接賓語，不接任何介詞。

reach 亦可解作「伸手去拿、伸手去觸摸」，這時要後接 for、into、out 等介詞。

實用例句齊來學

reach

- We **reached** the peak after five hours' walking.
  我們走了五個小時的路，終於到達山頂。

reach for / into / out

- She **reached for** the sugar and knocked over a glass.
  她伸手拿糖時，撞倒了一隻杯子。

- He **reached into** his bag and took out a gun.
  他伸手從袋子裏拿出一枝手槍。

- The girl **reached out** her hand to stroke the puppy.
  那女孩伸手去撫摸小狗。

增潤知識大放送

reach 可由 arrive at 取代，而在日常英語中，人們常用 get to 來表達相同意思，例如：

- We **reached / arrived at / got to** Shanghai late at night.
  我們深夜到達上海。

慣用語 reach for the stars 指「追求難以實現的東西」，例如：

- Make your dream into a burning desire. Don't be afraid to **reach for the stars**!
  把夢想變成一個強烈的慾望，心要比天高！

漫畫看一看

Mum, please sign here.

What's this?

I'll go to a camping trip this summer. The school needs your approval.

So you're going on a camping trip, right? Remember, we don't say "go to a trip."

Yes.

And we're planning to take a trip to the mountains. It's going to be fun!

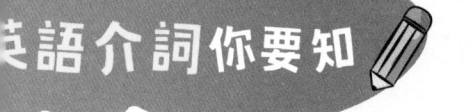

介詞解讀與辨析

go on a trip 或 be on a trip 都是指「出門旅行」，當中的介詞 on 不能説成 to。我們可以在 trip 前面加上修飾語，如 school、business、shopping、fishing、camping 等，以説明出門旅行的性質。

go on a trip 可以説成 take a trip，兩者意思相同。

實用例句齊來學

go / be on a trip

- Dad **is** away **on a business trip**. 爸爸出差了。
- Aunt Ruby **is going on a trip** to Tokyo.
  露比姨姨要去東京旅行。
- We will **go on a school trip** to Beijing this summer.
  這個夏天我們會跟學校去北京旅遊。
- Let's **go on a shopping trip** to Shenzhen this weekend.
  我們周末去深圳購物吧。
- They **went on a fishing trip** with the local fishermen.
  他們和當地漁民一起出發去釣魚。

take a trip

- We're thinking of **taking a trip** to the countryside.
  我們正考慮去鄉村旅行。

增潤知識大放送

make the trip 指「去旅行」，與 go on a trip 的意思相近，例如：

- He was unable to **make the trip**. 他無法成行。
- She did not have enough money, but was determined to **make the trip**. 她沒有足夠的錢，但決心要去旅行。

wait, wait for

英語介詞你要知

📢 介詞解讀與辨析

wait 解作「等待;等候」,作不及物動詞用。

wait 加上介詞 for 則要後接人物或事情,也可接時間。

★ 實用例句齊來學

wait

- "Have they arrived?" "No, I'm still **waiting**."
  「他們來了嗎?」「沒有,我還在等着。」

wait for someone / something

- **Wait for** me! 等等我!
- The children were **waiting for** the school bus. 小孩在等校巴。
- Robert was very nervous as he **waited for** the interview.
  羅伯特等候面試時非常緊張。
- Can you **wait for** five minutes?
  你能等五分鐘嗎?
- The singer kept us **waiting for** ages.
  那歌手讓我們等了好久。

🔍 增潤知識大放送

慣用語 wait a minute / second 指「等一下;且慢」,用於打斷別人的話,因為有不同意見,或突然想起重要的事情,必須及時說出。記住在這兩個慣用語中,wait 後不接介詞 for。例如:

- **Wait a minute!** That's not what we agreed.
  等等!那不是我們原先說好的。
- **Wait a second!** I forgot my wallet!
  等我一下!我忘了拿錢包了!

練習室 1

Choose the correct preposition for the following sentences. Tick the correct box.

請為下列句子選擇正確的介詞,並在 ☐ 加 ✓。

範例	Is there anybody (✓A. in ☐ B. on ☐ C. at) the room?
1	The girl ran (☐ A. off ☐ B. across ☐ C. opposite) the street.
2	They walked (☐ A. in ☐ B. under ☐ C. along) the river bank.
3	The train goes (☐ A. through ☐ B. by ☐ C. along) the tunnel.
4	She walked (☐ A. on ☐ B. around ☐ C. over) the building.
5	Tom is hiding (☐ A. under ☐ B. behind ☐ C. at) the door.
6	They ran (☐ A. against ☐ B. towards ☐ C. through) each other.
7	My grandparents live (☐ A. on ☐ B. at ☐ C. in) Guangzhou.
8	They are waiting (☐ A. at ☐ B. for ☐ C. of) the bus.
9	Don't throw stones (☐ A. for ☐ B. with ☐ C. at) the windows.
10	The old man lives (☐ A. in ☐ B. with ☐ C. at) his dogs.

練習室 2

Fill in the blanks with the suitable prepositon from the list given below.

請從下表選擇合適的介詞，填在橫線上。

about	between	during	from	inside
on	over	to	with	

We are going _____to_____ Singapore tomorrow.

The present is _____ the box.

He came _____ England.

Paul is playing _____ his brother.

They usually go _____ a morning walk.

We know nothing _____ the topic.

There was a long discussion _____ the teacher and the student.

I couldn't sleep _____ the flight. I feel very tired now.

Bill jumped _____ the fence to collect the ball.

練習室 3

There is a mistake in each of the following sentences. Circle and correct them in the spaces provided.

下列句子均有一處錯誤，請圈起錯誤的部分，並在橫線上寫上正確答案。

範例	Joseph's birthday is (at) October.	in
1	They will arrive on 3 p.m.	
2	The poem was written through Shakespeare.	
3	Please speak by Mandarin.	
4	Don't be late to school.	
5	There are some dirty spots over the floor.	
6	We need to drive across this tunnel to get to the other side of the mountain.	
7	Have you got a piece from blank paper?	
8	Brad repaired the bike by his friend's help.	
9	I have two model cars. What for you?	
10	She wore a diamond ring in her finger.	

參考答案：1. on → at 2. through → by 3. by → in 4. to → for
5. over → on 6. across → through 7. from → of 8. by → with
9. for → about 10. in → on / around

Fill in the blanks with the correct preposition for the following sentences.

請為下列句子填寫正確的介詞。

The painting is hanging _____on_____ the wall.

Cloth is sold _____ the metre.

The worker cut the timber _____ an electric saw.

Mom and dad are sitting _____ the couch.

Dad is _____ work at the moment.

The young boy sings _____ a professional.

The girl _____ long black hair is my cousin.

We've been reading books _____ this morning.

Lily came first in her class _____ everyone expected.

David ran _____ Charles to reach the finishing line in record time.

The young woman was employed _____ my father's secretary.

參考答案：1. by 2. with 3. on 4. at 5. like 6. with 7. since 8. as 9. past 10. by

133

練習室 5

There is one word missing in each of the following sentence Put a caret (∧) to indicate its place in the sentence and write the word in the space provided.

下列句子均有一個字詞不見了，請在相應位置加入插入符號（∧）並在橫線上寫上該字詞。

範例	We got out ∧ the car at the museum.	of
1	She took a book out her bag to read on the train.	_____
2	Sometimes I drink tea rather orange juice.	_____
3	This dish is made beef, red peppers and herbs.	_____
4	The chairman was absent owing illness.	_____
5	Six of ten visitors were from Asia.	_____
6	Eighteen divided six to get three.	_____
7	All her faults, we love her still.	_____
8	We went swimming spite of the typhoon.	_____
9	We were not allowed to go out because the bad weather.	_____
10	Lily got nervous when she spoke in front an audience.	_____

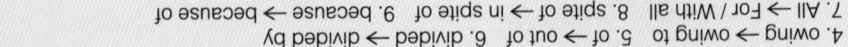

練習室6

There is a mistake in each of the following sentences.
Underline them and correct them in the spaces provided.

下列句子均有一處錯誤，請在錯誤部分下方畫線，並在橫線上
寫上正確答案。

The ship sailed <u>toward</u> the West.　　　towards

Come and sit here besides me.　　　_____

The baby was awake thank
to your shouting.　　　_____

The bus was delayed due of
the traffic jam.　　　_____

The bookfair was cancelled owning
to COVID-19.　　　_____

Four time four equals sixteen.　　　_____

What is 99 minu 33?　　　_____

We still enjoyed the weekend despites
the weather.　　　_____

She struggled though the crowd till
she reached the front.　　　_____

This plan goes again our interests. We
won't vote for it.　　　_____

You are free to keep the book untill
Sunday, but I must have it back on
Monday.　　　_____

參考答案：1. besides → beside　2. thank → thanks　3. of → to　4. owning → owing
5. time → times　6. minu → minus　7. despites → despite　8. though → through
9. again → against　10. untill → until

135

趣味漫畫學英語

小學漫畫英語王：Prepositions 介詞

作　　者：Aman Chiu
繪　　圖：黃裳
責任編輯：黃稔茵
美術設計：劉麗萍
出　　版：新雅文化事業有限公司
　　　　　香港英皇道 499 號北角工業大廈 18 樓
　　　　　電話：(852) 2138 7998
　　　　　傳真：(852) 2597 4003
　　　　　網址：http://www.sunya.com.hk
　　　　　電郵：marketing@sunya.com.hk
發　　行：香港聯合書刊物流有限公司
　　　　　香港荃灣德士古道 220-248 號荃灣工業中心 16 樓
　　　　　電話：(852) 2150 2100
　　　　　傳真：(852) 2407 3062
　　　　　電郵：info@suplogistics.com.hk
印　　刷：中華商務彩色印刷有限公司
　　　　　香港新界大埔汀麗路 36 號
版　　次：二〇二三年十二月初版

ISBN: 978-962-08-8291-3